That Dog Tarr

That Dog Tarr

(Original title: Tarr of Belway Smith)

by NAN HAYDEN AGLE

Illustrated by Barbara Seuling

SCHOLASTIC BOOK SERVICES

NEW YORK • TORONTO • LONDON • AUCKLAND • SYDNEY • TOKYO

ISBN: 0-590-04508-3

Text copyright ©1969 by Nan Hayden Agle. Illustrations copyright © 1969 by The Seabury Press. This edition is published by Scholastic Book Services, a division of Scholastic Magazines, Inc., by arrangement with The Seabury Press, Inc., original publishers of the book under the title TARR OF BELWAY SMITH

13 12 11 10 9 8 7 6   0 1 2 3 4 5/8
                    Printed in the U.S.A.   11

For Bill Alleman

Thanks to these people:
  Janet and Dick Tome, Edgar Benton,
  Edith and Arthur Hooper,
  Frances Bacon, Hilary Bacon 3d,
  Lillian Ballard, Laura Kassos,
  Jim Giblin, John Agle.

And thanks to these dogs:
  Toulouse, Molly, Keen, Little Jeff,
  Tarr Boy, Major, Jill, Kim,
  Polly, Pup, Brutus, Bob, Jack,
  The Hooper Dog.

Contents

Tarr and Monkton

TARR was a big, black Labrador retriever from Belway Kennels.

Everybody said he was the biggest, blackest, most beautiful dog around — his boy, Monkton Smith; Mr. and Mrs. Smith, the boy's father and mother; neighbors for five miles around the lake; strangers; and his friend Spot, a brown-and-white dog who lived under the bridge.

But nobody had to tell Tarr he was the greatest, most wonderful, most important dog anywhere. He knew that in the way he knew the lake was his to swim in, the woods was his to hunt in, the sun was up in the sky to keep him warm. And the yellow cat next door was his to hate and chase.

Right after lunch on Saturday, the first day of June, Tarr was asleep on the red rug in the living room, his black nose resting on the boy's feet. The boy's nose was in a book; his dark hair hung down over the rims of his glasses.

The boy sat perfectly still, reading, his long legs stretched way out to the middle of the red rug. Tarr's legs twitched now and then as he ran in a dream, chasing the yellow cat and gaining on her fast. Just as his mighty jaws were in snapping distance of her infuriating tail, a deep, loud voice woke him up.

Mr. Smith, smelling somewhat like an old leash, called to his son from the doorway, "Shut that blasted book, Monkton. You are always reading, and Tarr is always sleeping. You and he are two of a kind,

dreaming your lives away. Why don't you go out-side — ride your bike, or take a walk?"

Walk? Tarr leaped up, tail wagging, eyes shining hopefully. A walk with Monkton was almost as much fun as a rabbit hunt with Spot. Walk was a fine word, one of Tarr's favorites.

Tarr knew quite a few words. Living with people all the time, a smart dog is bound to pick up a large vocabulary. Tarr knew *walk, ride, go, stay, down, come, good dog,* and to his sorrow, *bad dog.* He also knew *sick 'em.* When rabbits got in the bean patch Monkton would say, "Sick 'em," and he would fly. So would the rabbits, their white tails bobbing as they hopped fast out of sight in the woods.

Tarr, of course, knew his name was Tarr. Mr. Smith, a sensible man, a teacher of math, called him Tarr. Nobody else did.

The boy called him Cerberus, Mrs. Smith called him Sweetie, and everybody else called him Blackie. It was upsetting to be called so many different names. Tarr wished everybody would call him Tarr. A dog liked to feel all in one piece.

The boy, who smelled wonderful, rich as a swamp full of muskrats, closed his book. He laid it on the table, flipped his hair back, and said to Tarr, "Come, Cerberus, great fifty-headed guardian of the infer-nal regions. Let us venture forth upon a high adven-ture."

Tarr didn't understand a word he said, but the tone

was happy and it made his tail wag faster. He loved Monkton more than hamburgers, more than beef bones or anything.

At the kennels, before Mr. Smith bought him, Tarr lived with a hollow feeling inside, like hunger only lonelier. Then Mr. Smith brought him home and gave him to Monkton as a present. Monkton greeted him, "Hail to thee, Cerberus," and right away the hollow feeling wasn't there any more. That was a spring ago.

By this time Mrs. Smith, smelling sweet as the lilac bush in full bloom, had come into the living room. She said to the boy in a dove-coo voice that made Tarr want to lie down and roll over, "Oh, Monkton, I wish you wouldn't talk that way. You *know* it upsets your father. You *know* Sweetie doesn't have fifty heads."

Mrs. Smith was not all lilac bush and dove-coo. She could make the best beef stew any dog ever tasted, and her pot roasts and steaks were drooling good. She fed Tarr twice a day at the back door, on time. Monkton was supposed to feed him and he did — choice tidbits of this and that under the dining room table. However, for regular meals, day after day, it was best to count on Mrs. Smith.

Now Mr. Smith banged his fist on the living room table and shouted, "The dog's name is Tarr, Tarr of Belway. It is written on his papers and printed on his name tag that is on his collar next to his license — Tarr of Belway. And he has *one* head."

Family squabbles always made Tarr want out. He

went to the front door at once and stood there waiting, his one head held high.

Presently the boy opened the door for him, saying, "Mind the moat, Cerberus, mind the moat," and followed him out on the porch.

Through the screen door Tarr heard Mr. Smith talking to Mrs. Smith. "Moat! What nonsense. This is not a castle. There is no moat around our house. That son of yours never faces reality, never. He never sees things as they are, never. I thought a dog would help him face facts. That's the main reason I got Tarr for him. But he has not improved one bit. In fact, by George, I believe that dog is fanciful too, and makes the boy more so!"

Tarr didn't get much of Mr. Smith's speech — just the word dog.

Tarr bounded down the drive.

It was a lovely day, sun shining, gentle breeze blowing, birds singing. Monkton followed him down the driveway, through the gate, down the lane, and up the trail through the woods. He was a tall boy, almost as tall as the young pine by the back door. And he was a fast walker, his long legs taking wide strides — but he couldn't keep up with Tarr.

Tarr ran on ahead, ears flapping. It had rained hard the night before, and the damp earth smelled wonderful. He stopped to wallow in a mud puddle. It felt good. As he shook himself, something moved under the sumac bush near by. He tiptoed closer, sniffing, full of expectation. A clumsy, fat groundhog waddled out and hurried away as fast as he could go, which was not a bit fast.

Tarr could have caught him easily and skinned him in no time if he'd had a mind to. He didn't though, just barked at him, "Rolf, Rolf," nosed him some, and let him go. Tarr was not a killer like his friend Spot. Spot killed to eat. He was a stray and he had to get food any way he could.

"Here, Cerberus."

Tarr dashed back to Monkton on the trail and for a short time kept him company. But people were so slow! Tarr couldn't stand it and raced on ahead again. A squirrel darted up a tree and sat scolding. Tarr went on, his tail high with pride.

At the top of the hill he sat down to wait for Monkton. Soon the boy came along, arms swinging, feet as muddy as Tarr's.

From the high hill, the highest point for miles around, they looked down on the lake below. On the far side of the lake sheep were grazing on a green hill. A lamb bleated, "Maaa, maa," over and over again. Tarr's sensitive ears could hear it. Monk's couldn't.

Below, on the near side of the lake, Tarr saw the Hoopers' big stone house and the horses in the pasture. He was staying away from there. Once when he and Spot were hunting they had crossed the pasture, and those horses chased them and tried to kick them. He and Spot had made it under the fence just in time.

"Look, Cerberus, sea monsters," said Monkton. He pointed toward the upper lake where ducks were swimming, one behind the other, in a straight line. Experience had taught Tarr it was practically useless to chase anything with wings.

For some time Monkton and Tarr sat together on a rock, hot in the sun, both contented with doing nothing. After a while Monkton got up and said, "Time to start back, Cerberus."

On the way home they took another trail, one that went by the crumbling foundation of an old house, burned down long ago.

"Buried treasure," said Monkton, digging with a stick in the earth beside the foundation. Tarr, feeling pretty sure a mole was down there, dug furiously, sending dirt flying out behind him.

Although Tarr was mistaken about the mole, Monkton found a treasure, a bottle the color of a dragonfly's wing. "Part of the crown jewels of the Empress of Austria," he declared, polishing the neck of the bottle with his sleeve. With the treasure in his pocket he walked on home, Tarr leading the way.

Monkton went into the house, back to his book. Tarr went into his doghouse in the breezeway to take a nap.

The nap was short.

Pad, pad, pad.

Tarr woke up, stuck his head out of the doghouse door and listened.

Pad, pad, pad.

Something was coming up the lane.

The Hooper Dog

TARR scrambled out of the doghouse, walked swiftly through the garage, and stood on the lawn, head held high, muscles taut under his handsome, shiny black coat.

PAD, PAD, PAD, louder now and nearer.

Tarr lowered his head and peered through the trees that lined the road. Something was coming, no doubt about that, and it was big. He could see it moving along.

PAD, PAD, PAD, loud and near!

Hackles rose along Tarr's backbone. What was it?

He barked a warning, "Rolf, rolf, rolf."

A deep "Roof, roof" with rumbling overtones answered him.

Tarr bristled. It was a dog, an enormous, sand-colored dog, big as a pony.

"Rolf, Rolf, Rolf!" Tarr warned the entire neighborhood in such a loud voice the Smith family came rushing out of the house to find out what was the matter.

"Rolf, rolf, rolf," Tarr kept on defending his property as he was supposed to do.

"It is the Hooper Dog," declared Mr. Smith, showing his teeth with pleasure.

Tarr never could understand why people showed

their teeth when they were pleased. Teeth were to scare the enemy and should be shown when you were *not* pleased. Any pup knew that much before he was weaned.

Mr. Smith went on, "I heard the Hoopers had a new dog, a big one, but I never dreamed he was *that* big."

"The Hooper Dog would make six of Cerberus," the boy said, and Mrs. Smith agreed, "At least six of Sweetie. That Hooper Dog is the biggest, most beautiful dog I have ever seen."

Tarr could not believe his ears. Another dog the biggest and most beautiful? He sulked. That hurt. He had always been called biggest, best, most beautiful, and blackest. Now he was just the blackest, and that was not enough. He sulked some more, glaring at the Hooper Dog who was coming through the gate by this time.

"Grrrrrrrrrr." Tarr showed his teeth.

"Be quiet, Tarr," scolded Mr. Smith. "Is that any way to greet a visitor?" And Mrs. Smith said, "Be nice to the great big dog, Sweetie. He's your new neighbor and friend."

Tarr got the message and did not like it. Then of all things, his own boy Monkton walked down the driveway to meet that Hooper Dog, patted him on the head, and called him "dragon, giant, minotaur," words of endearment that Tarr thought belonged to him.

Tarr growled again, "Grrrrrrr." Why was the Smith family so taken by that dog? He was big, no doubt about that — big, stupid, and muscle-bound.

Trembling with rage, Tarr stood beside the garage and watched the Hooper Dog come up the driveway almost to the house as though he lived there. Ignoring Tarr completely, not even glancing his way, that rude hulk of a dog strolled across the lawn, inspected the flower bed, the boxwood, and strolled back. Tarr watched him go down the driveway again, the Smiths complimenting him at every lumbering step.

Never had Tarr been so furious. He let the Hooper Dog get almost to the gate, then rushed him, and let him have it.

The earth shook, and trees trembled with reverberations of growls and snarls. Dirt and pebbles flew in all directions. First Tarr was on top, then the Hooper Dog, both of them snapping and growling.

Although the Hooper Dog was much bigger than Tarr it was a fair fight because Tarr was faster and smarter. Besides, Tarr was a pretty big dog himself and he was fierce when he had to be. And he was defending his own territory, which gave him twice as much power.

"Grrrrufff!" Pain shot through Tarr like lightning through a cloud. Blood ran down his leg. That blasted dog's long tooth had gone right through his hide. Tarr broke away, then seething with rage he lunged at the enemy with his head low. He danced to this side, to that side, trying to confuse the Hooper Dog, a slow thinker. Now was his chance. Head still low he came in fast under the bigger dog's heavy jaw, grabbed him by the neck where it counted, and held on.

He would have won the fight then and there, with honor, if people hadn't butted in and ruined everything. His own people, which made it worse. They had been hollering at him all during the fight, but he had been too busy to listen.

Wham! Monkton, his own Monkton, whacked him across the rump with a rake handle — his rump, not the Hooper Dog's. It was humiliating. And added to the hurt, Monkton kept yelling, "Desist, Cerberus! Halt before you slaughter the monster. You have thwarted him enough."

Wham! The rake handle landed on Tarr again, and he let go. His feelings were so hurt, much more than his rump. All the fight drained out of him. His own beloved boy, yelling at him, hitting him!

The Hooper Dog beat it fast down the lane, his tail between his legs.

Grumbling, still furious and hurt, Tarr dug up gobs of turf with his hind paws, sent them sailing through the air. At the same time he hurled insults after the fleeing enemy, "Grrrr-ruff, Grrrr-ruff!"

"Quit digging up the lawn," Mr. Smith shouted. "You are a BAD DOG, Tarr." And Mrs. Smith repeated, "Bad Dog, Sweetie."

Tarr winced. Being called a bad dog was worse than a wallop with a rake, worse than a wounded leg, worse than having his feelings hurt by his boy, almost. He would rather be whipped — not hard of course — than be called a bad dog. Anything but that. And here he had only been defending his own place, doing his duty.

He hung his head, feeling utterly miserable, looking pitiful, and not a Smith said a kind word. Instead they went back into the house, talking together about the Hooper Dog, the fight, and how rude Tarr had been.

"He nearly killed that dog, would have if you hadn't stopped him," Mr. Smith said to Monkton as the door shut behind them.

Tarr sat alone on the lawn feeling all mixed up. Everybody calling him a different name. The Hooper Dog showing up, much bigger than he was, and here all the time he'd been thinking he was the biggest dog anyplace. Now he didn't know who he was, what he was, or anything. On top of that, his own boy whacking him, his own people calling him bad dog. If he'd been a whiner he would have whined, but he wasn't.

It was such a lovely day. He and Monkton had had such a good walk. Then that Hooper Dog had to spoil everything. It was all his fault.

Tarr scratched vigorously with his hind paw and he didn't even have fleas. He scratched out of pure nervousness because nothing was right, not one thing. Oh, he had a good house to sleep in and plenty to eat, but everything else was out of joint. And it wasn't all the Hooper Dog's fault. The Smith's didn't have to side with him, a perfect stranger. They could have stood up for their own dog and should have. He was only doing his duty, dogwatching the place, taking care of things. And nobody appreciated it.

Tarr hurt all over, inside and out, and he felt very sorry for himself.

A bee zoomed over his head too close. Tarr hated bees almost as much as he hated the Hooper Dog and the yellow cat next door. He couldn't stand it around home a minute longer with everything and everybody against him. He would run away, that's what. The Smiths would be sorry they had treated him the way they had treated him, when they called him and he wasn't there. Yes, he would run away right now.

His sensitive ears heard a bird singing in the top of the dogwood tree, and way off a dog was barking. It sounded like Spot's voice.

Good old Spot. Now there was somebody you could depend on, somebody who appreciated you all of the time, not just some of the time. He would go find Spot, and they would run away together. He was pretty sure Spot would go with him because Spot did not have any home to leave, just a hideout under the bridge, no people of his own. Yes, he was pretty sure Spot would run away with him.

The wound under Tarr's hind leg hurt. He licked it and licked it, wishing the blood were the Hooper Dog's instead of his own. Now it felt better. He got up, stretched the leg to limber it up, then he loped across the lawn and headed toward the lake, not fast. There was no hurry. If you are running away, you have all the time there is to get to wherever it is you are going.

Danger

THE SHORTEST WAY to Spot's bridge was along the bank of the lake. Tarr loped through the woods down a narrow path he had made himself, leaves and underbrush close on both sides. In no time he burst out of the bushes, and there was the lake before him, shiny, rippling just enough to show it was alive. Being a retriever, a water dog, Tarr loved the lake.

He cocked his ear to listen. From the other side of the lake floated sounds of singing and laughter.

Tarr sniffed. The wind blowing his way was heavy with the delicious odor of hamburgers and smoke. A picnic, a Girl Scout picnic, judging by the high-pitched voices. Tarr had been to lots of Girl Scout picnics, and they were something a dog should not

28

miss, a normal, happy dog, that is. Today he was too sad for anything like that, and besides, running away was serious business.

He sniffed again. Those hamburgers smelled tempting, and a dog should not run away on an empty stomach. He would go to the picnic, then travel on to see Spot on the other bank with a full stomach. That was the sensible thing to do, and Tarr was a sensible dog.

He plunged into the cool lake and, with his black nose just above the water, dog-paddled expertly across to the other side.

"Here comes the big, black dog!" shouted one of the Scouts, a fat girl with short curly hair.

The rest of the girls, except a shy one with a pony tail, ran to meet Tarr. The shy girl ran up the hill and hid behind an oak tree, saying, "Don't let him come near me. He might bite."

Tarr scrambled up the bank and shook himself vigorously, showering the girls into giggles. One named Mary called out to the shy girl still behind the tree, "Come see him, Cathy, and pet him. He wouldn't hurt a fly. He's as kind as anything. See his tail wagging?"

Tarr wagged and sniffed. Smoke filled the air, almost drowning out the scent of hamburger, hot dogs, and girls —there was sort of an overripe peach odor to the bunch of girls.

Tarr was fond of all children, almost all. He had met a few he could do without. The thought of all children made him think of the most important one, his own boy, and he felt a pang of suffering. It didn't last long, though, for the picnic was about to begin.

It was a splendid picnic. Most of the girls sat around a wooden picnic table in the oak grove, eating, talking, and having a fine time while two older Scouts manned the grill and handed out fresh supplies. Tarr waited, standing at attention, mouth watering with expectation.

"Here, Blackie."

He ran around the table and gulped down half of a rare hamburger and a hunk of soggy roll.

"Here, Blackie."

He ran around to the other side of the table and swallowed whole a charred-black hot dog with mustard on it. If he'd known about the mustard in time, he would not have been so hasty.

Tarr went from Scout to Scout, eating and wagging his tail. For dessert he enjoyed an ice cream cone packed full of ice cream, very tasty, and a generous slice of chocolate cake.

While the girls stacked the paper plates and picked up the paper napkins, he cleaned up crumbs under the table.

Then everybody played games, including Tarr — catchers, I spy, and baseball. He was not too popular at baseball. He chased fielders and raced into the woods with the ball in his mouth, and all the girls chased after him, making as much noise as a flock of bluejays after a crow.

Everybody was having such a good time that nobody noticed the black cloud overhead until it opened up, and the rain poured down. Screeching like jays again, the girls ran to the boat dock to get out of the rain, with Tarr right behind them. They stayed there under cover talking and playing guessing games until somebody's father arrived in a blue station wagon to take them home.

"Go home, Blackie, go home," the girls told Tarr as they piled into the station wagon, holding boxes and bags and sweaters over their heads to keep dry.

Tarr did not go home. Feeling too full and very tired, he crawled under a rowboat that was upside down on the dock. In spite of the strong smell of fresh paint under there, he went to sleep.

When he woke up it was dark, and the rain had stopped. An owl close by called, "Hoo-hoo," and another owl off in the woods answered, "Hoo-hoo-hoo."

Tarr heard another call coming across the dark lake.

"Here, Cerberus, here, Cerberus!"

"Here, Sweetie!"

"Here, Tarr!"

His family calling him to come home. Part of him wanted to go at once, to mind as he always did. He was a good dog, used to minding. Another part of him, the hurt part, would not let him go.

It was too late to go on to Spot's bridge now. Night was not the time to run away. It would be much better to start out in the morning. Tarr curled up, tail pulled in, and slept all the rest of the night.

The next morning he crawled out from under the boat, sat on the dock and licked his wound. It was better, hardly bothered him at all. Then he set out. He did not swim back across the lake. Instead, he took the long way around the end of the lake, the land route to the bridge where Spot lived.

He walked swiftly with purpose down the center of the seldom-used railroad track where grass had grown thick between the ties, making a soft mat, easy on paws. Halfway to the bridge he met a brown dog, a stranger, coming up the track the other way. They eyed one another in passing but did not stop as both were out on business.

When Tarr reached the bridge he barked, "Rolf, rolf," for Spot.

Spot did not show up, so he barked again, louder. Still no sign of his friend. Tarr visited Spot's bed, way up under the bridge in the corner where bridge and road met. A strong smell of Spot was there. He must have just left to go hunting. One of Spot's favorite hunting grounds was on down the railroad track a way. Tarr would look for him there.

As he crossed under the bridge he noticed a car parked at the roadside with two men sitting in the front seat. One of the men opened the car door and spoke to him, "Hello, Blackie. Come here, fella, come here."

Being a well-mannered dog, Tarr wagged his tail politely. However, he kept his distance, for he had never seen the men before. They did not look a bit like Mr. Smith, the postman, the milkman, or any other man who ever came to the house.

The driver had strong horse shoulders and a sharp-nosed fox face. On his head was a sporty hat tilted to one side. The other man reminded Tarr of a ram he and Spot had met once when they were on the loose. No horns, naturally, but the man had a blunt ram nose and a ram look in his eyes.

"Nice Blackie," the blunt-nosed man said, holding out his hand, "Nice Blackie. Want a bone?"

Bone? Tarr knew that word for sure and he licked his lips with his long red tongue and wagged his tail faster.

"Get the nice bone," the man said, tossing something heavy onto the back seat and opening the back door of the car.

Tarr sniffed. He didn't smell any bone, only the strong smell of the strange men. What was that odor? It brought back a memory of the time he knocked a glass off of the coffee table in the living room at home. He knocked it off with his tail, and something spilled on the rug. People were there, guests of the Smiths, and they laughed. Mr. Smith did not say he was a bad dog, but he put him outdoors and would not let him come in again to get cheese on crackers, which he liked. Yes, those men smelled strong of the spilled glass.

Tarr kept his distance. He'd been trained not to get in cars with strangers. Mr. Smith said, "No, no, no," the time he got in a car full of children when they were shopping for groceries. Another time when a very nice man brought a package to the house he hopped in the truck with him and Mrs. Smith said, "No, Sweetie," and tapped him on the back with a newspaper.

Still, it would be fine to have a bone to take home

and bury in the parsley bed. No, he wasn't going home. He was running away. Even so, a bone to gnaw on would be fine, and the men must be good men to offer a bone to a dog they did not know. They must be very good men.

Tarr bounded over to the car and hopped in the back.

At once the door slammed shut behind him, barely missing the end of his tail.

Dognapped

Tᴀʀʀ liked to travel in his own car with his own people and he had traveled with them a lot. Let Mrs. Smith pull a suitcase out of the closet and he was ready to go. He'd been to Ocean City many times to swim in the ocean and chase seagulls along the wet beach early in the morning when dogs were allowed to run.

Traveling with these strange men against his will was frightening. Tarr did not know where he was going or what would happen to him and he did not like it a bit.

Still flat on the floor of the car, he listened to the dognappers talking together in the front seat.

"We've got this dog. Now what?" said one, and the

other answered, "We sell him as soon as possible. We've only got nine dollars left between us and a handful of change. The dog should bring us at least fifty bucks."

"Fifty? Labrador retrievers are worth twice that much!"

"Well, who we going to sell him to?"

"How about that man who deals in dogs? You know the one I mean — takes dogs without asking any questions and sells them to hospitals out of the state for experiments and stuff."

"I heard of him, read about him in the paper or something. Where's he live at?"

"Last time I heard he was fifteen or sixteen miles from here, out in the country. He runs a vegetable stand, or used to anyway."

"Okay. Let's go. What are we waiting for?"

Tarr suspected they were talking about him, but it was hard to guess what they were saying. Hoping to catch a word he knew, he lifted his ears slightly and kept on listening.

The driver said, "First we gotta get rid of his collar. We don't want a cop stopping us and catching us with a dog that don't belong to us and the evidence around his neck. Take it off and throw it away."

Tarr knew the word "collar." He was proud of his.

"*You* take it off. He might bite me."

"I'm driving. You do it. He won't bother you."

Without raising his chin off of the car floor, Tarr rolled his eyes up and saw the dognapper's hand appear over the back of the front seat. He growled, "Grrrrrr!"

The hand disappeared, and the man said, "I'm not losing an arm for any hundred dollars. You help me take it off or it stays on, cops or no cops."

The driver did not answer, just speeded the car faster. Soon afterward he stopped it in a wooded side road. Both men got out and walked around behind the car.

Tarr had to see what was going on. He got up on the seat and looked out the back window, his tail hanging down, the tip touching the floor. The men opened the trunk and took out a rope, a hatchet, and a tire iron. Then, while the fox-nosed man tied a knot in the rope, the blunt-nosed man went into the woods. Presently Tarr heard chopping, chopping, and soon the man came out again with a strong forked stick and a switch.

Before Tarr could hop down, the car door opened, and both men came at him at once. He backed into the corner, snarling and showing his powerful white teeth. He snapped at the forked stick thrust toward his neck but the men were too fast for him. One pinned his head against the seat and held it there with the stick under his ears while the other man took off his collar and slipped the rope in its place.

Wild-eyed, Tarr struggled to get free until the slip knot tightened around his neck, choking him. Then he stopped struggling and sat still. He had to. Nobody could win against a slip knot.

Tarr saw the collar land in the bushes. It was a pretty green collar with shiny studs, his name tag and license between the studs — a Christmas present from Monkton.

The car backed out and sped down the road again. Tarr sat upright on the back seat with the rope hanging down. He felt very sorry for himself. He felt angry too. If it hadn't been for the Hooper Dog he would be home now, safe, happy, eating his breakfast at the back door.

A wave of wanting to go home swept over Tarr and a wave of forgiving. He didn't forgive the Hooper Dog. He never would. He forgave the Smiths, especially Monkton. Tarr was a forgiving dog. He could not stay angry with his people or his friends. Even if Spot had been home and they had run away together, Tarr was sure they wouldn't have stayed away long.

He had to get home. He would break away from the dognappers the first chance he got and run home fast as a deer. He'd escape somehow. He'd watch and wait for a chance, then bolt. They couldn't keep him for long. He would see to that. Maybe he wasn't the biggest dog in the world, but he was the smartest and he would outsmart them.

The car slowed down at the crossroad, then speeded up again. Tarr heard church bells ringing. He saw cows peaceful in a field and horses standing in the shade by a stream and a white pony waiting at a gate. He saw a buzzard sitting on a fence, its dusty black shoulders hunched.

The dognappers didn't talk much. After quite a long ride the driver said, "Here's the place we're looking for," and he stopped the car in front of a rickety vegetable stand. There wasn't much on it, just a few boxes of strawberries, a couple of bunches of spindly asparagus, and some potatoes in a slat basket. Back behind the stand was a weather-beaten house, a shed leaning against it.

"Is your father around?" the driver asked a fat girl sitting on a wooden box, tending the stand, chewing gum fast.

"Pa!" she yelled, hurting Tarr's ears. "Some men to see you!"

The house door slammed, and a thin man with overalls much too big for him and a three-day beard on his chin came over to the car.

After some fast talk, the dognappers saying what a fine dog they had for sale, the man said, "I ain't in the dog business no more. A while back the S.P.C.A. put the law on me and run me out of business." He poked his head through the front window and looked at Tarr, saying, "Fancy hunting dog you got there." He spat tobacco juice fairly close to the potatoes and added, "As a favor, for a small fee I might be able to put you in line for a sale."

"We only got nine dollars between us and we got a date tonight."

"For a buck I'll keep the dog for you overnight and tell you the setup. You can't do nothin' with this deal on a Sunday. It's at a church."

"Church? How come?"

"The minister of a local church, E-piscopal church, has got himself a pack of hunting dogs, keeps them at his place behind the church."

"He hunt 'em?"

"*He* don't, but others do, them society people, horses, pink coats, and all. The minister just plumb likes a lot of dogs around. My guess is he'll take a fancy to yourn. Like I said, for a dollar I'll keep your dog until tomorrow and tell you where the church is at."

Reluctantly the driver handed over a dollar, and the vegetable man said, pointing across the road, "See that church steeple sticking up over the top of them trees?"

The dognappers nodded.

"Take the dog there tomorrow morning and chances are you can make a deal. Tie the dog to that tree for now. Come night, I'll shut him in the shed. You can pick him up when you are ready."

The next thing Tarr knew he was tied to the tree beside the weather-beaten house, and the dognappers had gone off and left him.

That was a long day and a longer night. Because of the slip knot, there was no possibility of getting away during the day. Tarr fumed and worried and remembered how he had been loved and cared for at home.

During the night, almost all night, he tried to get out of the shed. There was a wide crack between the wall and the floor, wide enough to get the end of his nose through. He pushed and pushed until his nose was raw and bleeding but he couldn't make the crack any wider. Then he scratched at the door until his paws were sore. The light of morning was showing through the crack when he finally dropped down exhausted.

An hour or so later he heard feet walking by outside. He got up and tried again, pushing his sore nose against the crack as hard as he could. It was useless. He couldn't get out.

The sun was halfway up the sky when the dognappers hauled him out.

"Look at him, a sore nose just when we want him to look fit. Dumb dog, trying to bust out. Come on!"

The blunt-nosed man yanked on the rope, and Tarr had to get back in the car again.

"Take the next dirt road," the vegetable man called to them as the car started. "It winds some and brings you to the back of the churchyard. Take it slow, it's bumpy."

The bumps nearly jarred Tarr's teeth loose and twice he slid off the seat. What a road! At least it was short.

In no time the car stopped in a pretty churchyard. The men got out and pulled Tarr out after them, the fox-nosed man saying, "Brace up, Blackie, quit drooping like you'd lost your last friend."

Tarr wanted to bite him in the leg but didn't.

Behind the little stone church Tarr was surrounded by a pack of friendly basset hounds all greeting him melodiously, tails wagging like wheat in the wind. Tarr did not wag his, although he knew he should for politeness' sake.

Hearing the dogs, the minister came out of the stone rectory. He was wearing gray pants, a white shirt with a round white collar, and a gray sweater open down the front. A pleasant-looking gentleman, one you'd never want to bite in the leg. In a loud, deep voice, hoping to be heard above the hounds, he greeted the dognappers and said, "That is a fine looking Labrador you have there," and he patted Tarr, showing a lot of teeth.

The dognappers answered louder still, "He's for sale. A man down the road said you might be interested in buying him."

"Thank you, no," the minister said, "I am a basset man, myself." His voice changed and he asked suspiciously, "Where did you get him? I see he is not wearing a collar or a license."

The men told a long story. Tarr could not follow it at all.

The minister nodded his head, only partially convinced, and said, "I've been reading in the paper about dognappers. It is a terrible thing to steal a man's dog."

"Terrible," agreed the two men. "Anybody who would do a thing like that should be put in jail."

"Rolf, rolf," Tarr barked, and the hounds started their singing again.

The minister leaned down and laid his hand hard on Tarr's head as he said, "You are indeed a fine fellow. Now let me think what would be best for you." He rocked back and forth on his heels, thinking, then said, "Perhaps the people at the Seeing Eye Headquarters might be able to use him. They train a few Labradors."

Tarr pricked up his ears. He knew a Seeing Eye dog. Mrs. Smith had a blind friend who had one called Sue. Once when the friend and Sue came to the house to visit, Tarr invited Sue to take a run with him in the woods. She would not go. She sat beside her blind charge and waited until she was needed.

The dognappers thanked the gentleman for his suggestion and said they would go there at once. They made Tarr get into the car, actually booted him in when he hung back and wouldn't move on his own.

The engine started, the bassets set up a musical good-bye, and Tarr and his captors headed back to town. It was quite a long way to the Seeing Eye Headquarters. Tarr crouched on the back seat, his body distorted by uneasiness. He could not sleep for dark thoughts and the tight rope around his neck. He wished he could get away, but he couldn't. The windows were closed, the door shut.

When they finally reached the Seeing Eye Headquarters the man behind the desk said, "We train female dogs only. They are more dependable, you know." He patted Tarr on the head and noticing his hangdog look, he said, "Somebody has been mistreating this dog. I know Labradors, and they are always friendly, happy dogs when treated right. I'll wager he could tell me a thing or two if he could speak. How about it, Blackie? How did you skin your nose?"

Tarr liked the man, recognized a friend. He managed a slight wag, and the man turned to the dognappers and asked, "Why do you want to sell him?"

They mumbled a string of talk about selling him for a fellow who had moved out of town and how they hoped to get a fair price for him as he was such a fine dog.

The Seeing Eye man patted Tarr on the head again and said, "Cheer up, fellow, the police department might sign you on as a K-9 recruit." He looked up at the dognappers and added, "Most of the K-9 dogs are German shepherds and Doberman pinschers, but a few are Labradors. Now if this dog of yours were a bloodhound, the detective department would snap him up. They are always looking for a good nose."

Tarr knew the word "bloodhound." He had met a bloodhound on the boardwalk at Ocean City the summer before, a large, loose-jointed melancholy dog. Mr. Smith had said over and over again that the dog was a bloodhound. Tarr recalled standing still, head up, tail out straight, while the bloodhound sniffed him all over, carefully as though he was committing him to memory. Tarr had been sniffed many times in his life but never so thoroughly.

The Seeing Eye interview over, the dognappers left, dragging Tarr after them. They did not go to the police station, however. Instead they stopped at a lunchroom, went inside, and left Tarr alone in the stuffy car.

He set up a howl at once, hoping somebody would hear him and come to his rescue. Nobody came. After a while the blunt-nosed man brought him a dish of water and a handful of table scraps. Hungry and thirsty as he was, Tarr refused to touch a thing.

Before long both men came out of the lunchroom and stood beside the car reading a newspaper, their heads close together.

"Hey, listen to this," one said, "Wanted — trained retriever, Labrador or Chesapeake Bay, good dis-

position, must like children. Call Edward Duncan, Chestertown, Maryland, 778-2668."

"That's for us. You'd better call Mr. Duncan right away before somebody beats us to it. There's a phone across the street in front of the drugstore."

The man talked quite a while. Tarr could see his broad shoulders inside the booth, his wide hat tilted

on his head. Then the man came back to the car stepping quickly, whistling as he walked.

"It's a deal," he told his companion. "We're to take the dog to Chestertown tomorrow. If he likes him, he'll pay a hundred bucks cash. And he'll like him."

"Good. What did you tell him about the dog? Will he ask questions?"

"I laid it on heavy about what a fine, well-trained hunter he was. We don't have a thing to worry about. Just leave things to me."

Tarr did not understand what was said but he knew the word "Chestertown." That word brought back pleasant memories of a happy day on the river with Monkton, Mr. and Mrs. Smith, and three cousins of his — three Chesapeake Bay retrievers. He remembered getting home late at night. He'd never forget it. A deer crossed the road right in front of the headlights, but Monkton would not let him chase it. He shut him in the breezeway all night. First thing in the morning Tarr had gone straight to where he had seen the deer. But there was no sign of him except deer tracks, holding in them a wild, fair scent that kept Tarr hunting, nose to the ground, all day until he nearly dropped.

That night with the dognappers Tarr was tired from being upset, from trying to get out of the shed the night before, from not enough to eat. Still, he could not sleep. He was tied to a tree at the edge of a woods, he didn't know where, the two dognappers lying on the ground close by. The moon was full, and a full moon always made him restless even when he was in his own doghouse.

He sat up, pointed his nose at the moon and howled, "Wooooooo!"

"Shut up, dog."

A stick or something whizzed past his head and landed on the ground beyond the tree.

"Woooooooooo!"

One of the men got up, came over to Tarr and slapped him rudely in the face, saying "Shut up." He did loosen the slip knot, which helped some.

Tarr curled up, nose under his hind leg, and pulled in his tail. He wondered what would happen tomorrow. One thing sure: when they got to Chestertown, he was going to break away somehow and get back home. He had to get back to Monkton.

Finally Tarr went to sleep and dreamed. The dream was not a happy one of chasing the yellow cat. It was vague, full of shadowy things he could not see or smell.

Sold

THE NEXT MORNING Tarr ate a light breakfast. He was so hungry and thirsty he couldn't turn down the dog biscuits and water the men offered him. His legs were so stiff he didn't turn down a short brisk walk, either — across a field by the woods and back to the car, pulling hard on the line the whole time.

"His nose is better."

"Some. At least it's not bleeding anymore."

The two men boosted Tarr into the car, one hauling on the rope, the other shoving from behind.

"Clamp his jaws shut with a loop of the rope and hold it while I brush him off. He's got himself plenty dusty."

"No. Leave him be. He looks okay."

"For a hundred dollars he's got to look sharp. A hundred bucks! Sounds good, don't it?"

"I'll say, and the sooner I get my hands on my half, the better. We got enough left for gas and nothing else. Let's go. Sooner we get there, sooner we get the money."

The car headed south, traveling miles and miles through little towns, along country roads, over bridges, through more little towns.

Part of the time Tarr looked out of the window feeling solemn and lonely. Home had been so comfortable, more than he knew when he was there — love, good food, care, and Monkton. He saw a brown-and-white dog that reminded him of Spot. Yes, he had friends at home too. He sighed.

He lay down on the seat and dozed, not really sleeping, just half awake, keeping one eye on the men in the front seat.

When the sun was directly overhead the travelers reached Chestertown. Tarr could smell the river out of sight somewhere. It smelled good. He stuck his nose out of the crack in the window and sniffed. Yes, it smelled very good. After Monkton, Mr. and Mrs. Smith, and Spot, he loved water best of anything.

"Which way to the Duncan place, Mr. Edward Duncan's?" the driver asked a young man pushing a lawn mower.

"About a mile down that way, white gateposts on

the left-hand side of the road. You can't miss it, large white house set back, lawn in front with mimosa trees, and a shady driveway."

It didn't take the car long to go the mile, go through the white gate, down the shady driveway, and come to a stop in front of the large white house.

The driver got out, went up the steps, crossed the wide porch, and rang the doorbell.

"Mr. Duncan is expecting us," he told the maid who opened the door.

She saw Tarr sitting bolt upright on the back seat of the car and raised her voice to call out, "Mr. Duncan, the men are here with the new dog!"

Mr. Duncan came out on the porch at once. He was shorter than Mr. Smith and thicker, with gray hair on his head and under his nose. He smelled like a clean, well-groomed horse, somewhat like Mr. Smith. Dear Mr. Smith. Tarr licked his lips twice, slowly, sorrowfully, missing the Smiths so much, mostly Monkton.

"Fine dog you have there," Mr. Duncan said, peering at Tarr through the window. "Largest Labrador retriever I have ever seen. He is all you said he was over the telephone and more."

"Yes, sir, he's a beauty," one of the dognappers said, and the other opened the back door and pulled Tarr out, a reluctant Tarr, not looking his best, tail between his legs, head low, hate looking out of his eyes.

"You are sure he is a well-trained hunting dog?" asked Mr. Duncan, feeling Tarr's left hind leg as though he were buying stewing beef.

"Yes, sir, trained on Kent Island by one of the finest dog trainers in the state of Maryland. He's a good house pet too, gentle with children."

"Splendid, splendid. What is his name?"

"Blackie."

"Well, Blackie," Mr. Duncan said, showing a row of large white teeth, "how would you like to be my dog from now on?"

Although Tarr did not understand the words, from the tone of voice and the teeth he was pretty sure the man had said something pleasant. Grateful for that, he wagged his tail slightly and his eyes warmed up a little bit.

"Good," Mr. Duncan said, patting him on the head. "Blackie and I are going to get along fine. My old dog Belle hunted with me for fifteen years, best duck retriever I have ever seen. She died a month ago, and I am lost without her. We all are. That is why I put the ad in the Baltimore paper. No use advertising for hunting dogs around here. Everybody wants to keep them if they are any good. Speaking of papers, you have Blackie's papers, I presume?"

Lies filled the air. Tarr could feel them in his bones. The dognappers went on and on about how Blackie belonged to a soldier and how they didn't like to bother the soldier's wife about the dog's papers and how they would mail them to Mr. Duncan before long.

Mr. Duncan nodded his head. He handed the men ten ten-dollar bills, and they handed Tarr over to him and that was that. Tarr was Mr. Duncan's dog, sold, paid for, and delivered.

Because he was a careful man, Mr. Duncan jotted down the license number of the car as it started down the driveway.

As Tarr watched the car taking those dognappers out of his life forever he growled, "Grrrrrrr," and Mr. Duncan said, "I didn't think much of them myself, Blackie. Come along with me and meet my family. You will like them, and they will love you."

Bang!

Tarr followed Mr. Duncan into the house, the rope slack between them. Before he had a chance to inspect the front hall two young boys and two young girls came thundering down the stairs, all shouting at once, "Where is the new dog? We want to see him."

At the same time a woman, taller and slimmer than Mrs. Smith, came to the living room door and said, "Children, children, not so loud. You'll scare the dog with your racket. Dogs have sensitive ears."

"My family, Blackie," Mr. Duncan said with a wave of his hand. And pleased as a robin with a fat worm he said to the family, "This is Blackie, our dog."

The words "our dog" had a familiar ring. Tarr had heard the Smiths call him that. He couldn't be the

Duncans' dog. He was the Smiths' already and for always — Monkton's dog.

Mrs. Duncan said something, but he could not hear what it was because the children were jumping up and down, jabbering about what a wonderful, great big, black dog he was. When Mr. Duncan said, "You can pet him. He won't hurt you," they fell upon Tarr like a batch of eager pups, patted him, and hugged him around the neck, shouting, "Blackie is our new dog, Blackie is our new dog!"

The youngest, a roly-poly girl, crawled under his belly and came up on the other side, bubbling with laughter. The next to youngest, a boy with red hair, sang out, "Don't you wish Belle could see him?"

The older children took turns saying, "Take the rope off of him." "Give him something to eat." "Give him some water to drink."

When Mr. Duncan explained that Blackie could not run free until he was used to his new home, the oldest boy said, "Well then, put Belle's collar and leash on him and let's take him outdoors and show him around. The collar's in the pantry, hanging on a nail. Belle wouldn't mind Blackie wearing it."

"Yes, let's do," the other children said together, and the next to oldest boy fetched the collar and leash at once.

Belle's collar fitted Tarr perfectly, not too loose, not too tight. It wasn't fancy like his own green collar

with the shiny studs that was lying somewhere in the bushes, but it was much better than a rope with a slip knot.

Before going for the walk, everybody stood in a circle around Tarr in the kitchen while he lapped up a bowl of milk and ate a plateful of meat scraps. As soon as he had licked the plate and his lips clean they all went outdoors, Mr. Duncan holding the leash.

They visited the barn, the chicken house, the garden, the cornfield, and the meadow where lots of cows were grazing. Two horses were in the meadow too, and a goat. Beyond it, behind a row of willows, was the river. Tarr could see it glistening, moving. A good place for a swim.

Tarr decided the Duncan place would be a fine home for a dog if he didn't already have one. Especially for a water dog, a hunter.

"Tomorrow we will go for a trial hunt," Mr. Duncan said as they started back to the house, the children walking as close to Tarr as they could get, their hands resting on his back. "Hunting season does not open until fall. Still, we can get the feel of a hunt and see how we work together. What do you say, Blackie?"

Tarr looked up at Mr. Duncan and wagged his tail. He liked the man's pleasant tone of voice saying the good word "hunt." Tarr considered himself to be just about the best hunting dog anywhere, a natural-born hunter with a keen nose. Anything that ran he chased for the fun of it. He was not the trained hunting dog the dognappers claimed he was, however. He had never had a hunting lesson on Kent Island or anyplace else. A smart dog did not need hunting lessons and he was a smart dog, very smart.

That night Tarr slept peacefully, stretched out full length on a folded rug under the kitchen table, two windows wide open to let in the fresh air. At sunup Mr. Duncan woke him, and the two of them set out on the trial hunt. A rope long enough to give Tarr plenty of room to roam was hooked to Belle's collar, his collar now. The other end of the rope was tied around Mr. Duncan's waist so Tarr could not roam too far and get away. Mr. Duncan carried a gun under his arm, the barrel pointed down toward the earth.

They crossed the back field and walked down to the swampy land by the river, Tarr leading the way. A small brown bird went with them, flitted from tree to tree, twittering about something on its mind. Tarr breathed deeply, filling his handsome wide chest. He loved the smell of the early morning world, everything cool and wet with dew. He wished for Monkton. If he had been there, everything would have been perfect. Without Monkton nothing was any good, nothing at all.

Mr. Duncan stopped near a willow tree on the riverbank and called to Tarr softly, "Come, Blackie."

Tarr ran to his side, and Mr. Duncan motioned toward the water with his free hand, saying, "Wait until fall, Blackie. You'll see hundreds of ducks and geese out there then. We'll have a grand time together. I'll shoot, and you'll retrieve."

He leaned down, holding the gun in front of Tarr's nose. Tarr inspected it carefully with interest, ears raised slightly. The smell of gunpowder was new to him, strong and rich. It stirred the roots of his hair along the backbone.

Then Mr. Duncan raised the gun to his shoulder, aimed out across the river toward the woods on the far side, and pulled the trigger.

BANG!

Tarr fell to pieces. His four legs went in four different directions. Trembling all over so his teeth chattered aloud, ears deaf from that terrible bang, he shot straight up into the air and bolted.

Wham! The rope jerked him to a stop. Mr. Duncan on the other end of the rope took a tumble.

"Gun shy! A gun-shy dog! I've been gypped!" he exclaimed as he got to his feet.

Tarr pulled, yanked, dashed up, dashed back, twisted, turned, frantic to get loose. He pulled so hard Mr. Duncan dropped the gun and slid along the ground yelling, "Blackie, Blackie, no, no, wait!" Somehow the rope caught on a tree trunk and held.

Now Tarr all but threw a fit. Head this way, that

way, paws digging into the soft earth, he pulled and pulled and pulled.

Slowly Belle's collar came off over his head, a tight squeeze, his ears nearly coming off with it.

Free at last!

Tarr lit out for home, straight across the field. He passed the Duncans' house and sailed down the driveway, tail out straight, legs flying. He tore through the gate and raced down the road the way he had come with the dognappers. No dog ever ran faster. He never slowed down or looked back, just ran and ran as fast as he could run, tongue hanging out, eyes wild, the whites showing.

He was a long way from home but he would get there. Nothing would stop him now. He was on his way. He ran and ran and ran.

People stepped aside to let him pass. Cars slammed on brakes to let him cross streets. He ran and ran and ran, that BANG ringing in his ears. He ran all day long through country places, through little towns, across lawns, through woods, straight for home.

At night he was exhausted, dusty, thirsty, and so tired he could hardly stand up. He stopped, panting, panting. He lifted his ears and above the sound of his own panting he heard water running, a lovely cool tinkling sound of a stream. Gratefully he waded in under a little bridge, lapped and lapped the cool water. He stood still, cooling his burning paws. He squatted and let the water run over him. He wallowed in the mud until he began to feel soothed and comforted.

Lap, lap, lap, he drank more. The panting had almost stopped now. Then, never so tired in his life before, he lay down on the healing mossy bank and slept.

The moon came out and did not disturb him. A raccoon came down to the water to drink, and Tarr did not stir. A snake slithered right across his tail, and he did not wake up, he was so tired.

When morning came his empty stomach gnawed on his insides, demanding food. He had to get something to eat. Without making a sound he padded along the bank of the stream a little way until he saw a rabbit nibbling grass. He leaped upon it before it had a chance to flee, killed it instantly, skinned it, and ate it, bones and all — something he did not do as a rule except sometimes in dreams.

Now he was ready for the day. He ran back to the road and headed for home. He loped along swiftly, at an even pace, not running wildly as he had the day before. A steady even pace was best. He kept well over to the side of the road, nose straight ahead, eyes and ears on the alert.

When the sun was high, he came upon several men sitting behind a truck parked at the roadside, workmen eating lunch.

"Here, Black Dog," one called out to him, offering him part of a sandwich.

Not ever again. Tarr was not going to trust a strange man ever again, not after the dognappers and that BANG. Home was the only safe place. Your own people were the only ones to trust.

He ran on. After a while a small dog chased after him, yapping and yapping at his heels. Tarr did not stop or even turn around. In a town some boys about Monkton's size tried to catch him. He had to detour down a side street and cut back to the main road to lose them.

In the late afternoon he stopped in somebody's yard for a drink of water from a fish pond. He did not see two girls in a lawn swing beside the house but they saw him. While his head was down drinking, the girl with pigtails ran quickly to the gate and shut it so he could not get out. The other girl ran to the house shouting, "Mother, come look. We caught a big dog with no collar on. May we keep him?"

Wild as a wolf, Tarr ran around inside the fence, looking for some way out. Finding none, he backed off and tried to jump the fence. He almost made it but missed, the palings were too high. As he was about to try again, a running jump, the mother of the children appeared. She sized Tarr up at once and said, "Let him out, girls. He must be lost. A big, black Labrador like that surely belongs to somebody. Open the gate at once."

Tarr dashed through the gate as it swung back and ran on until sundown. Fortunately he found an old barn not far from the road, a perfect place to spend the night. He made himself a nest in the hay, curled up in it, and slept pretty well in spite of a mouse who kept scurrying around making a nuisance of itself.

Sunup he was on the road again.

He made good time during the morning. But around noon, while crossing a railroad track, he cut the center pad of his right front paw. It was a mean cut. He licked and licked and licked it before it would stop bleeding. When he finally got under way again he had to limp, and now and then go on three legs, which slowed him up. Every so often he had to stop to lick the wound clean and ease it.

He was getting hungry again by this time, having had nothing to eat since the rabbit. He got hungrier and hungrier as he traveled on. When he was limping past a farmhouse not far from the road he stopped in and robbed the garbage can by the back door, something he had never done before.

All he could find was a mess of chicken bones, not much of a meal for a hungry dog. Still, it was better than nothing. Somebody opened the kitchen door, yelled at him, "Get away from there, you dog," and threw a bucket of water at him. Luckily it missed as he skidded out of the way and ran off.

For a short while he covered ground at a fairly good speed, then the sore paw began to bother him so he had to stop and ease it. He crawled under some bushes in a thicket at the roadside, out of sight. Here in the cool shade he licked and licked some more, not an easy thing to do when you are panting hard. He listened to cars going past. Two men walked by, talking together. Tarr watched them through the leaves and smelled them. They did not see him hidden in the bushes.

It was lovely there, resting, but he had to go on. He could not really rest until he was safe in his own dog-house. He came out of the bushes and traveled slowly on three legs, holding up the sore paw. After a while he began to put it down for a few steps and finally he eased it into a steady, fairly fast limpy run.

At last he reached a long bridge, the bridge leading into the city. He stopped for a moment before crossing, to savor the fishy smell of the harbor. Home was on the other side of town. Maybe tonight, tomorrow for sure, he would sleep in his own doghouse, he would be with Monkton and Mr. and Mrs. Smith. That is, if all went well.

The Dog Pound

Tarr crossed the bridge, dodging cars going both ways, drivers yelling at him to get out of the way, horns honking.

At the first stop light on the edge of town a lasso came down over his head; the loose ring of the noose slipped tight. It all happened so quickly he didn't have a chance to put up any fight or even back away or growl.

"Easy, boy, easy. I'm not going to hurt you," a heavy-set man said, looming up at Tarr's side. To a man close by, the deep voice said, "Give me a hand with him, Gustave, he is a big fellow."

DOGCATCHERS!

"Grrrrrrr!"

Before Tarr could growl a second time the two strong men hoisted him bodily into the back of a truck and shut the solid wire door behind him.

A middle-sized fuzzy dog with hair over his eyes was there already, along with a pup who insisted upon chewing on Tarr's hind leg as though they were in some happy meadow.

A dirty white dog, a female, was on the other side of a wire partition. Tarr peered at her through the diamond-shaped mesh. She was a sorrowful dog, scared as a trapped rabbit, with a hurt, unloved look in her eyes. From the way she was scratching she had plenty of fleas.

Tarr did not have fleas but he was scared and his paw burned and throbbed. As the truck went down the street, swaying from side to side, it was all he could do to keep from bumping into the fuzzy dog and stepping on the pup.

The truck drove through a desolate part of town where Tarr had never been before. Windows and doors of row houses were boarded up. Stray pieces of newspaper blew along the empty sidewalk. For blocks and blocks Tarr did not see a living soul except one lonely old man, brown as a tree trunk. He was sitting on a step, leaning wearily on a cane.

Mr. Smith had a cane. Sometimes Monkton borrowed it and swung it jauntily as he and Tarr walked down to the mailbox for the morning paper. Tarr won-

dered when he and Monkton would go for the paper again. It was not going to be easy to get away from the dogcatchers, not a bit easy. They were not dog-nappers, stealing dogs to sell. They were experts with a job to do, picking up stray dogs.

Before long the truck stopped in front of two low red-brick buildings trimmed in dark grass-green. A sign — MUNICIPAL ANIMAL SHELTER — hung over the office entrance. Between the two buildings, holding them together in one unit, were high, wide, dark-green double doors.

The doors opened. The truck drove through. The doors closed, and Tarr was in the dog pound.

"Yap, yap, yap!"

"Arf, arf!"

"Yip, yip, yip."

"Roof, roof!"

A jumble of barks greeted the truck from dog runs on both sides of an open courtyard. The yard and all of the runs were spotlessly clean. Too clean to suit Tarr. He preferred an earthy smell to that of soap. Still, it was better than a dirty smell, much better.

Some runs had a bunch of dogs in them, others only a few. In several runs there was only one dog. Most of the dogs were alike in appearance, tan coats, mid-dle-sized, slim, nervous, pointed noses, rather large ears and long tails. They all had an admirable eagerness in tail and eye, a wish to be noticed and liked which impressed Tarr.

That handsome dark German shepherd standing alert in a run by himself was a somebody. What a stance he had. Tarr felt a slight twinge of envy seeing him.

The barking stopped almost at once, and the dogs down at the run gates, tails wagging, watched the yardman unload the truck.

The pup was lifted out first and put in the puppy run with an assortment of other pups who greeted him with enthusiasm. A sign over the puppy gate said in large letters — FOR ADOPTION.

The yardman, swift as a deer, collared the fuzzy dog with a short loop of rope, whisked him out of the truck, and dipped him in a bathtub in the center of the yard, a tub full of something smelly.

What was that odor? A memory stirred deep in Tarr. He and Spot were across the lake, over where the ram lived. They were in high grass watching sheep being dipped.

The timid white dog was dipped next, which all but finished her off, she was so scared. However, once she was in a run with several other females she revived enough to make it to the far corner.

Tarr, last to leave the truck, waited, holding up his sore paw. It really hurt a lot, more than licking could cure.

"Put this one in isolation until the vet looks at his paw," the yard foreman said, looking in at Tarr.

Any other time Tarr would have liked the man—sandy hair, kind face, sensitive eyes, soft voice. Right now he wasn't liking anybody or anything.

"Come on, Smoke," the yardman said, pulling Tarr out with that loop of rope as easy as chasing a squirrel up a tree.

Smoke, another name. Tarr, Cerberus, Sweetie, Blackie, and now Smoke.

Tarr limped with dignity to his run, the yardman leading. The man opened the run gate, and Tarr went in bravely, head up, without a boost from the rear, conscious that the German shepherd was watching from his run directly across the courtyard.

Tarr sat down on the clean concrete and scratched furiously with his right hind paw. Fleas! Ouch, another one bit him.

The yardman must have noticed the scratching, for he hauled Tarr right out of the run and dipped him in the tub. He fought like a tiger, flaying the air with all fours, but in he went, up to the eyes, and out again. After shaking himself he had to admit he felt better, tingling all over.

Back in his run he sat down and recalled the time the Smiths gave him a bath in their bathtub. He had had a slight encounter with a skunk, and Mrs. Smith

said he could not come in the house unless he had a
bath. So Monkton filled the bathtub and all three
Smiths put him in. Then while Mr. and Mrs. Smith
held him, Monkton soaped him. Full of white lather,
he had leaped out of the tub, raced to the kitchen and

out the back door, sending rugs flying behind him, lather spattering in all directions. It took a lot of rolling in the woods to get rid of the soap and days of living outdoors to lose the last reminder of the skunk.

A wave of homesickness swept over Tarr, a painful longing. He'd had everything any dog could wish for: boy, home, love, good food, admiration, everything — and he had lost it all. If only he had been dog enough to take a bit of discipline, he would not be in the pound now.

He was in jail and he could not get out. No dog could. Concrete floor, brick wall halfway up, heavy wire the rest of the way. No dog could dig under or climb over.

The yardmen were kind. He had his own clean white drinking basin with running water. He had his own clean dinner plate. He had other dogs around him.

But he couldn't get out.

At the far end of the generous run was a little dog-high door with a flap of canvas hanging in front. Tarr pushed the canvas aside and went into his private cell. It was about two dogs long and two dogs wide. A shallow wooden box for a bed was there and another door to the inside hall. Standing there in the dim light, loneliness overwhelmed Tarr. Door to the hall closed, gate to the run closed, big green doors to the courtyard closed and locked.

"Rolf, rolf, rolf, rolf, rolf!" He barked and barked until he was hoarse, then he went out in the run and barked some more until he noticed the shepherd dog looking at him, ears pointed, eyes sharp.

That evening Tarr found out who the shepherd was. He was Sherlock, the night watchdog. He belonged at the Animal Shelter and ran free all night. He and the night yardman worked together, making the rounds, checking the kennels, keeping an eye out for prowlers. No wonder Sherlock was so keen. He had a job to do. He was free.

Tarr wished he was free, guarding the Smiths' house, taking care of Monkton, keeping the yellow cat and the Hooper Dog well out of sight. He licked his paw and listened to the sounds around him: pups playing, a dog whining, the yardman's footsteps as he went from kennel to kennel, Sherlock running swiftly here and there. He raised his ears hearing the sound of whimpering in the adjoining run. He stood on his hind legs and looked over the brick wall through the wire mesh. A sick, pitifully thin dog was there, lying on its side. Tarr felt sorry for it and for himself.

The next morning the poor sick dog was gone, and Tarr never saw it again. Several other dogs disappeared that day too. Tarr wondered what became of them. Not knowing made him feel uneasy.

Shortly after the yardman hosed out Tarr's run, the vet came. He was a young man who smelled ever so faintly like Monkton, just a shadow of Monkton's scent, enough to make Tarr lick his lips slowly twice, remembering.

The doctor examined the sore paw, painted it with dark medicine that made it sting. Next he put on a bandage the size of a hornet's nest and wound it tight with yards of adhesive tape. Tarr spent the rest of the day trying to get the bandage off. He couldn't, but trying took his mind off of his troubles.

Three long, dreary days later the vet put on a fresh dressing, a smaller one, and said, "You'll be fine soon, Sport."

Would he ever be called by his name?

Tarr paced in his cell, three steps up, turn, three steps back, turn, on and on. He drank water. He ate the food the yardman brought in a wheelbarrow and shoveled into his clean dish. Although the food was not as tasty as Mrs. Smith's beef stew, it was not too bad. He had tasted worse and it was served every day on time.

Days passed slowly for Tarr. He wondered about his friends, the fuzzy dog, the pup, the white dog, what they were doing, how they were standing being in jail. One day he saw the pup go by in the arms of a girl. The pup was wriggling with delight, waving its small tail. The girl was glowing. So the pup was lucky.

Another day he noticed the fuzzy dog out in the yard, jumping up and down, barking and acting silly. Then he watched him leave, pulling a boy on a rope. So *he* was lucky too.

Other dogs left the shelter with other people. Some dogs disappeared mysteriously without people, there one day, gone the next. New dogs arrived in the truck. But Tarr and the white dog stayed.

Once a man wanted to take Tarr home with him but his wife said, "That big dog in a third-floor apartment?" and they walked away.

By the time Tarr's paw had healed, his spirits were low, very low. He was listless and didn't care much about anything. When he thought about Monkton and home it wasn't real, not a live boy and a real home, just a formless ache.

One day followed another, all the same: wake up, the run hosed out, sleep, dinner, more sleep, night-time, more sleep, no fun, very little hope.

The yardman put another dog in the run with Tarr to cheer him up, a short-haired, short-tailed dog called Brownie, nervous as a mother cat. Brownie made Tarr nervous too, the way he ran up and down panting, getting nowhere. He was glad when they moved Brownie to another run.

Tarr became so discouraged he could not eat. He got thinner and thinner, sadder and sadder. He slept most of the time, dreaming horrible dreams.

"We might as well put him to sleep," the yardman said to the yard foreman one morning as the two of them were standing outside Tarr's gate.

"Not yet," the foreman answered. "He will be the next DOG OF THE WEEK. The newspaper reporter and photographer will be here today to take his picture and write his blurb for the paper."

"Smoke, DOG OF THE WEEK!" exclaimed the yardman. "It's a waste of time. The white dog's picture was in the paper last week, and it didn't do *her* any good. She is still here. The black dog is done for, if you ask me. He's had it."

Tarr had had it, no doubt about that. He heard the men talking, didn't listen, didn't care what they said. He didn't care about anything anymore. Not one thing.

The yardman had to prop him up to have his picture taken when the newspaper reporter came around noon. Tarr would not perk up his ears or look the least bit bright. And as soon as the camera clicked he slumped down and slunk back into his cell, out of sight.

"Black dog, male, Labrador retriever type about two years old, may be yours for five dollars," the reporter wrote down in his notebook. It wasn't much of an advertisement but it was all he could gather from his interview with Tarr. Before leaving, the young man added one more line, "Telephone CE 3-0200 or visit the Municipal Animal Shelter and see Smoke for yourself."

Dog of the Week

The following afternoon Tarr, DOG OF THE WEEK, was lying half asleep in the outside run, his back toward the gate.

"There he is, Henry," a woman's voice said. "See him lying there. My, he is a big dog. Let's take him, Henry. A Labrador for five dollars is a bargain."

"Feeding him wouldn't be," Henry answered. "A dog that size would eat us out of house and home. Why not take the terrier in the next kennel? He is peppy and won't eat much. Come on, Stella."

Footsteps moved away, but Tarr just lay there. Presently he heard more footsteps and a vaguely familiar voice said, "I want to see your DOG OF THE WEEK. My gun-shy Labrador ran away from home a month or so ago. Today, my wife and I brought the children up to town to the dentist. We were sitting in the dentist's office waiting for the children, reading the paper, when I noticed your DOG OF THE WEEK. We think he may be our Blackie."

Mr. Duncan from Chestertown! Tarr got to his feet and began to shake all over, remembering that dreadful BANG.

"That's Blackie," Mr. Duncan said, peering through the gate. "Here, Blackie, here, boy. Poor fellow. He doesn't look a bit well."

"I'm glad he is your dog," the yardman said. "He is pining away. A sore paw kept us from advertising him when we first picked him up. He is a well-bred dog. We hoped we would not have to put him to sleep. Come, Smoke."

The yardman opened the gate, flipped that little rope, and dragged Tarr out into the courtyard. Then he dragged him to the office, the white dog and Sherlock both watching. Tarr, way beyond pride, had to be boosted bodily through the door to the Animal Shelter Office.

Once there, things happened so fast Tarr could not tell which came first. The Duncan children were petting him, calling him "Poor dear Blackie, poor thin Blackie." The man at the desk and Mr. Duncan were discussing money. Mr. Duncan, his wallet out, was counting dollar bills, "One, two, three, four, five,"

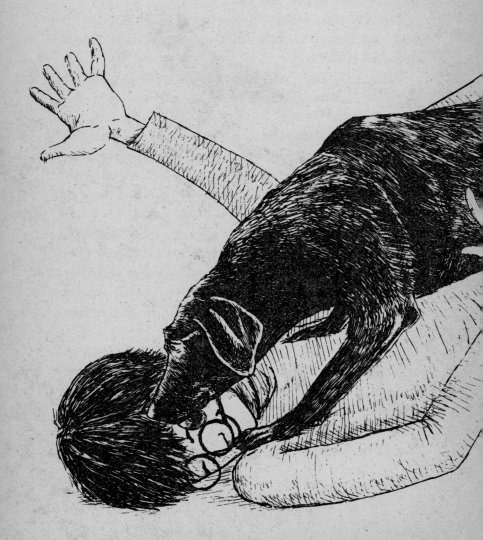

when the outside door opened and in came Mr. and Mrs. Smith and Monkton.

Monkton, Tarr's own Monkton, real, live Monkton. long legs, eyeglasses, swampy smell, tennis shoes—glorious Monkton!

With one wild joyous leap Tarr landed on the boy, spilling the Duncan children in all directions. Monkton went down with a thud, Tarr on top of him, licking his face, licking tears from his cheeks, and Monkton saying over and over, "Tarr of Belway Smith, my own Tarr."

Not Cerberus — Tarr of Belway Smith he called him. His own boy calling him by his own name.

Everybody talked at once, Mrs. and Mr. Smith saying they came as soon as they saw Tarr's DOG OF THE WEEK picture in the paper, the Duncan children saying, "He is not Tarr. He is our Blackie, and *we* came as soon as *we* saw his picture."

Monkton, still flat on the floor, arms around Tarr, said, "We tried to find him, we looked for him everywhere — police, radio, television, S.P.C.A., the Humane Society. We called here as soon as he went away but nobody had seen him then. Nobody anywhere had seen him. We thought we had lost him forever."

In the middle of the hubbub Mr. Duncan tried to console his children by saying, "Look at the dog and the boy. You know they belong together. You can tell by the way they met. You know he is the other boy's dog. Don't you?"

The Duncan children nodded sadly, and the oldest said, "Then get us another dog, Daddy. We want Blackie, but another dog will do."

"Yes, another dog will do," repeated the other three. "We *need* a dog at our house."

Mr. Duncan hastily told the Smiths about the dognappers and about Tarr being gun-shy and running away when the gun went off. Then he declared in an angry voice that he'd catch those dognappers if it were the last thing he ever did and he'd get his money back and buy a good hunting dog. After he cooled down he turned to the yardman and said, "Pick out a dog for my children, any dog looking for a good home."

"We'll go with him and help pick it out," the children said, lining up in front of the yard door ready to go.

"Oh, no," said Mr. Duncan, shaking his head, "not you four. You would want every dog in sight. You wait right here with your mother and me." So the children waited impatiently while the yardman went to fetch them a dog.

To Tarr's joy the yardman fetched the timid white dog in his arms. She was too scared to walk. Tarr thought she looked pretty, all clean, white, and fluffy. The Duncan children thought so too. They named her Snow at once and surrounded her with bountiful, noisy love.

Tarr, fairly bursting with love and happiness himself, left the Animal Shelter with Monkton and crossed the street to the Smiths' car. Mr. and Mrs. Smith were not long in coming.

The ride home was joyous for the whole Smith family, including Tarr. Monkton kept hugging him, calling him Tarr, not Cerberus, the fifty-headed dog, not once. Mrs. Smith called him Tarr too, not Sweetie. She and Mr. Smith kept saying how much they missed him, how sorry they were about the fight with the Hooper Dog and all.

Although Tarr did not understand everything they said, he got the gist of it and wagged his tail. As soon as the car stopped in front of the garage he leaped out, his joints creaking from lack of exercise.

And who should be sunning himself on the front lawn but the Hooper Dog!

In spite of feeling weak and wobbly in the legs, Tarr chased that dog down the driveway and part way down the lane, and nobody scolded him or told him he shouldn't. On the way back to the house he took it slowly, he was so winded. At the gate he stopped and sniffed. Spot had been to see him. Good old Spot. Tarr would see him soon.

He walked slowly up the driveway, taking his time, walked through the garage to the breezeway and went into his doghouse. As he did, a yellow streak shot out over his head, the yellow cat from next door, ye-owing with fright, her tail three times its natural size.

What a nerve. That cat in *his* house. What a nerve!

"Here, Tarr, here, Tarr, supper!"

That was Monkton calling from the back door, Monkton calling him to supper, not Mrs. Smith. Tarr got there pretty fast considering, gulped down rare roast beef with delicious gravy, and licked the plate clean. Monkton stood beaming down at him.

Mr. and Mrs. Smith beamed at him too, over Monkton's shoulder, and Mr. Smith said to Mrs. Smith, "The boy has his feet on the ground at last. No more dreaming his life away in fantasy, and it was Tarr that did it."

"It was the almost losing Tarr that did it," Mrs. Smith said. Then Mr. Smith said he would give anything to know Tarr's whole story, where he had been, what he had done and all. Mrs. Smith said she would too.

Monkton said, "He is home again and that is all that matters." Then he picked up the empty plate and went into the house.

Tarr followed him through the kitchen, along the hall, and into the living room. Monkton sat down in his chair beside the table and reached for his book.

Tarr lay down on the red rug close by and rested his black nose on the boy's feet.

The boy smelled so good, better than a swamp, better than deer tracks, better than beef bones or anything else anywhere. It was so good to be home with him again. Only a dog who had been away for a long time could possibly know how good.

While he was away from home Tarr had learned that he wasn't the biggest, most important dog in the world — maybe he wasn't even the blackest and most beautiful. He didn't have to be. He was Tarr of Belway Smith, a big, black, gun-shy Labrador retriever. As for being gun-shy, no dog is perfect.

He was a wise dog now, wise enough to know that part of the outside world was grim and frightening but not all of it, wise enough to know that all of home was good, even an occasional whack when he needed it. Getting to be a wise dog was worth everything that had happened. Almost everything anyway.

Monkton turned another page, and Tarr of Belway Smith went to sleep.